MARIANTHE'S STORY
ONE

Painted Words

ALIKI

GREENWILLOW BOOKS, NEW YORK

Colored pencils and crayons were used to create the full-color art. The text type is Korinna BT.
Library of Congress Cataloging-in-Publication Data: Aliki.   [Marianthe's story: painted words]   Marianthe's story: painted words ; Marianthe's story: spoken memories / by Aliki.   p.   cm.
Summary: Two separate stories in one book, the first telling of Mari's starting school in a new land, and the second describing village life in her country before she and her family left in search of a better life.   ISBN 0-688-15661-4 (trade).
ISBN 0-688-15662-2 (lib. bdg.)   [1. Schools—Fiction.   2. Storytelling—Fiction.]   I. Title: Marianthe's story: spoken memories.   PZ7.A397Mar   1998   [Fic]—dc21   97-34653   CIP   AC

For those dedicated, unsung teachers
who change and enrich lives

Marianthe knew this day would come.
Now that it was here, she didn't know
if she would laugh or cry.
"I won't know anyone," she said again.
"Most people don't know anyone at a new school,"
said Mama.
"I won't understand what they say," said Marianthe.
"You will look and listen and learn," said Mama.

"They won't understand me," said Marianthe.

"A body can talk," said Mama. "Eyes speak many words,
 and a smile is a smile in any language."

"Everything here is so different," said Marianthe.

"Only on the outside," said Mama.

"Inside, people are the same."

"I am a little afraid," said Marianthe. "But not enough to cry."

Marianthe felt hot and frozen at the same time.

She did not understand when the tall teacher said,

"We are delighted to have you, Marianthe.

May we call you Mari?"

But she understood when he bent down and shook her hand.

She did not understand when he said,
"This is our new teammate, Mari,"
or when the children said, "Good morning, Mari."
But she understood when he led her to her own desk,
and when some of the children smiled, and others waved.

The tall teacher wrote words on the board.

They looked like sticks and chicken feet, humps and moons.

Mari could just look.

He read from a book.

Words changed with his voice.

They sounded like sputters and coughs and whispering wind.

The words made the children laugh, and say "ahhh" or "ooh."

Mari could just listen.

Suddenly everyone jumped up and scattered around the room.

Some piled blocks into towers.

Others lumped clay into shapes or threaded pasta.

"Misapeechi," Mari heard.

"Misapeechi. Misapeechi," she heard again and again.

Each time the teacher answered, and Mari understood.

This was his name.

Misapeechi swept the air with his arm,
and again Mari understood.
She went straight to an easel and began to paint.
"Mari is an artist," said Rachel.
"High marks for observation," said Misapeechi.

The next day Mari looked and listened.

During Creating Time, she painted again.

"Mari is telling us something," said Albert.

"She is talking with her paints," said Rachel.

"There's more than one way to peel an orange," said Misapeechi.

"And there is more than one way to tell a story. Someday Mari will be able to tell us with words."

Every day when Mari went home,
Mama listened and learned.
She heard about the many different things
that were becoming familiar to Mari—voice sounds
and counting numbers and writing those funny sticks
that were also in the schoolbooks they read.
"And every day I draw another picture," Mari told Mama.
"It's my story about us.
I am drawing what I can't talk."

Mari told Mama of tall Misapeechi,
and of Waisha and Kista and Ahbe,
who smiled and spoke with their eyes
and talked with their hands so she could understand.
And she told of the other ones.
"In life there will always be those who hurt and tease
out of ignorance," said Mama.
"You look and listen so you will not be one of them."

Patik was the worst.
He snickered and nudged and whispered
and shouted "Dummy" whenever he could.
Mari could see from his face what "dummy" meant.
That day she was hurt enough to cry, but she didn't.
She painted instead.

That day everyone understood Mari's painting, even Patik.
"We have here a great deal to talk about," said Misapeechi.
"Let our ideas begin."

Slowly, like clouds lifting, things became clearer.

Sticks and chicken feet became letters.

Sputters and coughs became words.

And the words had meanings.

Every day Mari understood more and more.

Misapeechi became Mr. Petrie.

Waisha became Rachel, Kista became Kristin,

Ahbe became Albert, and Patik became Patrick.

One day Mr. Petrie clipped a heap of paintings to the wall.
"The time has come for patience to be rewarded," he said.
"Ready, Mari?"
"Ready," said Mari.
She told her story in her new words,
page by painted page, as she would read a book.

When she finished, the class clapped and cheered.

"Bravo!" "More!" they shouted. "We want more!"

"We shall have more," said Mr. Petrie.

"I have a strong suspicion that we have here
a class of writers, each with a story to tell."

"I have one," said Kristin.

"I have one," said Patrick.

"And we'll call our classroom Writers Galore."

Mari was so excited, her heart skipped beats
as she told Mama.
"And look at you, Mama," she said.
Mama was writing in her book,
copying letters into words into meanings.

"You have looked and listened and learned well, Mama,"
said Mari.
"Soon you will be writing your own story.
Just think what Mr. Petrie will say!"